Artie

and

Merlin

Artie and Merlin

by Sue Ruff & Don E. Wilson
illustrations by Lolette S. Guthrie

Tenley Circle Press
Washington, D.C.

CATALOGING IN PUBLICATION DATA
Ruff, Sue.
Artie and Merlin.
Wilson, Don E.
Guthrie, Lolette S.

ISBN: 978-0-9773536-2-0

Library of Congress Control Number: 2009901848

Tenley Circle Press, Ltd.
P.O. Box 5625, Friendship Station, Washington, D.C. 20016
www.tenleycirclepress.com

COVER ART: Lolette S. Guthrie

BOOK DESIGN: Margaret Allen Earley

LUCIDA GRANDE FONT (body type), LUCIDA BRIGHT FONT (display type).
Designed by Charles Bigelow & Kris Holmes

PRINTING & BINDING: Beacon Printing Company, Inc., Waldorf, MD, USA

*Beacon Printing Company enforces a strict recycling program
and is committed to worker safety and health as an integral
part of its business plan. Beacon is SFI (Sustainable Forestry
Initiative) certified and uses paper from responsibly managed
forests and other controlled sources. The inks used in printing this book are vegetable based, not made from petroleum
products.*

For our grandchildren

Carly and Julia Bowers
Alison and Lindsey Filbey
Kimaya Guthrie
Sammy, Tommy, and Clarissa Wagner

Contents

~ ONE ~

Artie's Dream

Artie stretched one leg at a time and opened his eyes. The sky was pink. The birds were twittering. It was a beautiful morning, not too hot and not too cold. The air was stirring the leaves on the trees in the farmyard.

Suddenly something flew into the yard and landed in the tree over Artie's head. It was Merlin. Artie sat up. "Oh," he thought. "It would be fun to be a bat!"

"Merlin! Merlin!" he called. "I want to be a bat, too!"

Merlin was tired. He had been out all night. He didn't want to talk to anyone, not even Artie. "You can't be a bat," he grumped. "You don't have claws."

Artie looked at his hooves in surprise. Of course he didn't have claws. Pigs don't have claws. "What do claws have to do with it?" he asked.

"You have to sleep. Everyone has to sleep. I sleep hanging upside down by my claws. That's what bats do."

Merlin held onto the tree with one of his hind feet and waggled the other one. "See?" he asked.

Artie rubbed his nose with his hoof. "Maybe I can learn to fly anyway," he said wistfully.

"Artie, look at yourself. You're shaped like a table. Even if you had wings, you couldn't flap them."

"I don't see why not," Artie sighed.

Merlin spread his wings and flapped in a slow circle above Artie's head. "Look how my arms are connected to my body," he said. "I'm shaped more like a person than a table."

Artie could see the bat's arm and hand bones inside the thin skin of his wings. The delicate bones reminded Artie of the veins of a leaf. "Merlin's right," the pig thought sadly, looking down at his own sturdy legs. "I can't move my legs the way he moves his when he flies. I really am shaped like a table. I can't move my legs sideways."

Merlin roosted again and folded his wings. He yawned and closed his eyes.

Artie had a lot to think about. He flopped down on the ground in the shade of the tree. He yawned. He yawned again. A minute later, he was fast asleep.

Soon Artie was dreaming. At first it was a good dream. He dreamed that his neck grew longer and longer. He nibbled a leaf from the treetop. He peeked into a bird's nest. This was fun! He wasn't flying, but at least his head was up high.

Artie smiled in his sleep. He rolled over, but he didn't wake up. He continued to dream, but his dream changed. It got scary.

Suddenly Artie wasn't himself any more. He was a little animal with a long, bushy tail. He was running as fast as he could through the branches of the tree. He was running ... and running.... Something was chasing him! He tried to jump to another branch. He was falling...!

Artie woke up with a squeal of terror.

His squeal woke Merlin. "Artie, you had a bad dream, didn't you?" he asked.

Artie nodded.

"You look sad, too. Is that because I can fly and you can't?"

Artie nodded again.

"But Artie," said Merlin, "I can't walk. I can't even stand up. I can cling to things, and I can crawl a little bit, and I can fly. You can walk and run!"

Artie was surprised. He looked up at Merlin and asked, "If you can't stand up, how can you eat your dinner?"

It was Merlin's turn to look thoughtful. "I have to grab it on the fly," he said, "one bug at a time."

"We're awfully different, Merlin," said Artie.

"But we have lots in common, because we're both mammals."

"What do you mean? What do we have in common?" Artie asked.

"When you were a baby you drank milk from your mother's body. So did I. Did you know baby bats nurse upside down?"

"Upside down?" Artie exclaimed. "I wonder if I could drink upside down! What else?"

"We both have hair. My hair is soft and silky. Yours is short and bristly. But it's hair. Only mammals have hair."

Artie rubbed his bristles against the tree. Then he carefully stretched each leg, one at a time. They were strong and made for running. He ran in three big circles around the yard. He stopped to munch an apple. Then he gave his tail a happy twitch.

Merlin looked down wistfully at his friend. "You know what else?" the bat asked. "I can't twitch my tail. It's almost completely inside my tail membrane."

Artie thought about how good the apple tasted. He couldn't imagine having to chase his dinner. He couldn't imagine eating insects. He couldn't imagine sleeping hanging upside down. He looked up and asked, "Didn't you ever want to be a pig, Merlin?"

"Not really," Merlin said, "but I really do want to sleep." He closed his eyes, and soon he was dreaming about wallowing in mud.

Artie was wide awake. He looked around for something to do and saw two squirrels chasing each other. They were running up and down and around the trunk of a big oak tree. Artie trotted over to watch them. "How can squirrels run headfirst down trees without falling on their noses?" he wondered. "When Merlin wakes up this evening I'll ask him. Maybe he knows."

~ TWO ~

Hanging Around Together

As soon as Artie woke up the next morning, he looked for Merlin. He saw his friend in the big tree in the farmyard where the bat usually roosted during the day.

"Hi, Merlin," Artie called. "What are you doing?"

"Just hanging around," laughed the bat.

Actually, Merlin planned to hang around sleeping. But he was hungry. "I had a bad night, Artie," he said. "It rained all night. There weren't any bugs flying around, so I missed my dinner."

"Want some of my food?" asked Artie. He knew that Merlin ate insects every night. He had never thought about what happened to his friend when it rained.

"No, that's okay," said Merlin. "It's clearing up. I'll pig out tonight."

Artie laughed. He loved to eat, and he loved the expression "pig out." But something about the bat's voice worried Artie. "Are you extra-extra-very-very hungry, Merlin?" he asked.

"Actually, I am. Fall's coming. I have to hibernate soon. Before I do, I have to gain a lot of weight," said Merlin.

"What on earth are you talking about?" asked the pig.

"I spend the winter asleep," said Merlin. "Doesn't everybody?"

"You'll miss Christmas!" Artie cried.

Merlin had always slept through Christmas—and Kwanzaa and

Hanukkah—so he didn't know what Artie was talking about.

"Where will you go? What will you do?" the pig cried.

"I have to find a cool, safe place," Merlin said. "An attic would be a perfect place to hibernate. A cave would be good, too. I need a place that's cold, but not freezing. I need a place where I won't get rained on or snowed on."

"But *why?*" Artie wanted to know.

"Because there's not enough for me to eat in the winter. I'd starve. Some bats fly miles and miles every fall. They go someplace where it's warm and buggy. Then they fly all the way back to their summer roosts in the spring. But not me. I just sleep through the winter. Sort of like a bear."

"I'm going to try it," said Artie. He flopped down, burrowed his snout under a pile of hay, and closed his eyes. A minute later, he opened one eye. "This isn't much fun," he said.

"Napping isn't hibernating. When I hibernate, all sorts of things happen. Things you can't do."

"Like what? What can't I do?"

"My whole body gets cold. As cold as the air around me," Merlin explained. "My heart slows way, way down. I barely breathe. And I don't eat the whole time.

My body just uses up its own fat. By spring I'll be so skinny, you might not recognize me!"

Artie immediately gave up all thought of hibernating. He had no desire to miss even one meal, let alone a whole season of meals. "When will you go?" he asked.

"I'm not sure, " Merlin replied. "When I'm fat enough. When the nights are chilly. When the days get short. When there isn't enough to eat. At some point I'll just know it's time, and I'll go. But I'll say good-bye before I leave."

"Will you come back?" asked Artie.

"Of course I will. I promise."

"I'm going to miss you, Merlin. Who will I talk to?"

"Me," said a soft voice. "You can talk to me!"

Artie spun around and saw an animal with a white face, a pointy nose, and two bright eyes. It was Mrs. P, the opossum.

"You can talk to me," she said again. "I'll be around all winter. And when spring comes and Merlin is back, I'll show both of you some really cute babies." She shuffled off toward her den in the woods.

"She's so nice," said Artie when Mrs. P had gone. "But if she's an opossum, why isn't her name Mrs. O?"

Fortunately, Merlin knew why. "It's a nickname for a nickname, Artie. 'Possum' is a nickname for 'opossum,' and Mrs. P is her nickname." Merlin yawned and added, "I have to get some sleep. I have to hunt tonight. Have a good day."

21

"I'll be very quiet so you can sleep, Merlin," promised Artie—who saw a butterfly, snorted noisily trying to catch its scent, and stumbled after it.

~ THREE ~
The Best Defense

Merlin woke up just as the sun was setting. He yawned, opened his eyes, stretched his wings—and saw two animals coming toward him. Melissa, the skunk, was coming out of the woods on his left. Folly, the bloodhound, was snuffling her way across the yard on his right. Melissa didn't see Folly. Folly didn't see Melissa.

"Stop!" Merlin shouted. "Folly, stop!"

"Huh?" said Folly. She was only half-listening. Her nose was down and her wrinkles hid her eyes. She was following an interesting scent.

" STOP!" Artie echoed—but Folly kept coming.

Melissa and Folly came closer and closer. And then—

"Oh, hi, Melissa," said Folly.

"Hi yourself," replied Melissa. She walked right under Folly, tickling Folly's tummy with her tail, and continued on her way toward the woods.

Merlin sighed with relief. "I was sure she would spray you!" he said.

"Oh, no, we're friends," replied Folly. "She sprayed me once when I was a puppy, but now she knows I won't hurt her."

"What happened when she sprayed you?" asked Artie.

"It was awful. I saw her in the woods and went bouncing up to meet

25

her—and she got me! My eyes watered. I was gasping for breath." Folly laughed at the memory.

"Didn't she give you any warning?" asked Artie.

"She did. She stamped her feet. Then she stuck her tail straight up in the air. But remember, I was just a puppy. I didn't know what she was trying to tell me, and I ran right up to her."

"I was sure she was going to let loose," Merlin said. "But I guess Melissa has a right to defend herself if she thinks she's in danger."

"Everyone does," said Folly. "The first time I met her, she had a litter of kits. You can't blame her for protecting them. I'm the friendliest dog around, but if I had a litter of puppies, I wouldn't let you or Artie get near them."

Mrs. P walked up while Folly was talking. "Remember the first time we met?" she asked.

"No," said Folly. "What happened?"

"You were so obnoxious. You thought everything in the world was a toy for you to play with. Including me."

"But what happened?" asked Folly. "I really don't remember."

"I was a lot younger, too. I was only about half the size I am now," said the opossum. "You came bouncing up and barked at me. I was terrified. I played possum—"

"I remember!" said Folly. "You fell over on your side. You were as stiff as a plastic Frisbee! I picked you up and carried you around in my mouth."

"Finally you got bored, I guess. You put me down and went away." Mrs. P shook her head at the memory. "I got up and went back to my den. What a night! It was a long time after that before I came down out of a tree if you were around."

"I'm glad I didn't hurt you," said Folly. She lifted her head and sniffed the air. Something smelled interesting.

"I have to go," she said. "See you later. Don't go near any strange skunks!"

"Is it true that she didn't hurt you?" Merlin asked Mrs. P.

"She slobbered all over my fur. I was a mess! It took me ages to finish grooming myself. But no, she didn't hurt me. She has a very gentle mouth. A very big mouth, but a very gentle mouth."

Suddenly Mrs. P twitched her long, pointed nose. "What do I smell?" she wondered. "I think it's pizza! I think there's pizza in the garbage can. Maybe that's what I'll have for dinner. Good-bye, Merlin. See you later, Artie."

Mrs. P shuffled off, and Artie turned

to Merlin. "What do opossums usually eat, Merlin?" he asked.

"Oh, almost anything," Merlin answered. "Fruit, nuts, worms, snakes...."

"Worms! Uck!" To change the subject, Artie asked, "Who do you think has the best defense, Mrs. P or Melissa?"

"Oh, Melissa, without a doubt," the bat replied. "When an opossum 'plays possum,' it seems to be dead. Other animals will usually leave it alone, but I'll bet a skunk's spray could even stop a hungry wolf. And guess what? Baby skunks can spray when they're only a week old. They don't even have fur yet. Their eyes aren't even open yet!"

"I hope I never get sprayed. Good luck hunting tonight, Merlin."

"Thanks, Artie. I have to start looking for a place to hibernate, too. It's just about time. Sleep tight."

~ FOUR ~

James

Winter came, and Artie was lonely. He missed Merlin. Sometimes he talked out loud, even though Merlin wasn't there to hear him. "I just love to rub my short, bristly hair against the fence," he said, suiting his action to his words.

"I suppose you think your hair is special," said a voice.

Artie jumped straight into the air,

landed, and spun around three times. Who could be talking to him on this cold morning? He didn't recognize the voice.

Then he saw an animal shuffling slowly out of the woods.

The animal came close to Artie and stared at him. "Well?" it asked.

Artie stared back. He didn't know what to say.

"When it comes to hair, I have you beat by a mile," the strange animal said.

Artie took a cautious step closer. "I don't think you have any hair at all," he said, "except maybe for a little bit on your face."

"Wrong, wrong, wrong," said the stranger. "Listen to this." The animal shook, and Artie heard a rattling noise. "Every single one of my quills is made of hair."

Artie liked almost everyone, but he wasn't at all sure he liked this boastful creature. "What are you?" he asked. Merlin would probably know, he thought, but Merlin was hibernating.

"I am a rodent," the animal declared. "A huge rodent. I'm a porcupine. Most rodents are little things. Mice and voles. Squirrels. But who cares about them? I'm big and fearless. I have one of the best defenses in the Animal

Kingdom." The porcupine turned and started to shuffle back into the woods.

"Wait!" Artie shouted. "What did you mean about having one of the best defenses?"

"My quills. Each one is as sharp as a needle. If a fox or a coyote tried to eat me, it would get a mouthful of quills." The porcupine sounded much less grumpy because he saw that Artie was really interested.

Artie shuddered. He didn't like to think about animals eating other animals. "What would you do?" he asked. "Would you throw your quills at a coyote?"

"No. Porcupines don't throw their quills. That's what people think, but they're wrong. I just turn around backwards and swat my enemy with my tail. That's all it takes."

"Awesome," said Artie. "What's your name?"

"I don't know," said the porcupine. "I live alone and no one speaks to me much."

"You need a name," declared the pig. "Are you a boy or a girl?"

"I am a male," said the porcupine. "A boy."

"I'm a male, too!" said Artie,

twitching his own little tail. "My name is Artie. Maybe I could call you James. Do you like the name James? Can I call you James?"

Before the porcupine could answer him, Artie continued, "Have you always had those quills?"

"Suit yourself," said the newly named James. "I was born with quills. They were soft when I was born, but they hardened in a few hours. I was born with my eyes open, too, and I already had teeth. I could eat by myself when I was only about a week old."

"But you were only a tiny baby!" Artie exclaimed. "What did you eat? What do you eat now?" he asked.

"Nice green grass stems in the summer. Corn, in the fall. I love corn! And tree bark now, in the winter."

"I love corn, too," Artie squealed, glad that he finally found something they had in common.

"You know," said the porcupine, "You really are a very nice animal. Is there anything I can do for you?"

"May I have one of your quills?" asked Artie.

"What are you going to do with it?" James asked.

"I don't know," Artie said. "Just keep it. Look at it. Think about it."

The porcupine grinned a great big porcupine grin. "Okay," he said. "Stand back."

Artie moved away from the fence, and James backed carefully up to it.

He swatted his tail at the fence. "That's called tail-flailing," he said. "I love to say it. Tail flail! Tail flail! Tail flail!" He smiled at Artie again and shuffled back toward the woods.

The fence was full of quills. Artie couldn't wait to show them to Merlin and tell him about James. "Oh," he sighed. "I hope spring comes soon!"

~ FIVE ~

The Pig Family

The days were getting a little bit longer and a little bit warmer. The trees were starting to bud. The birds were thinking about building nests. Artie thought about Merlin. It must be almost time for him to finish hibernating. Suddenly he heard a voice say, "Hi, Artie."

It was Merlin! Artie looked up. He didn't see his friend.

"Hi, Artie!" Artie heard Merlin's voice again.

"Where are you?" demanded the pig.

"I'll give you a hint," said Merlin. "Bark."

"Woof!" said Artie.

The hint worked, but not the way Merlin thought it would. When Artie barked, the bat laughed so hard he shook all over. Artie's eyes caught the movement, and he saw Merlin clinging to the bark of a tree.

"Pretty funny, Merlin," said Artie.

"That was camouflage," said Merlin.

"What was?" asked Artie.

"The way I blended into my surroundings so you couldn't see me. A hungry hawk flying overhead couldn't see me, either. As long as I hold still, my camouflage works."

Artie looked at his reflection in his water bucket. "I don't think I have camouflage," he said.

"You're right, Artie," replied Merlin. "You're a domestic animal. A farm animal. Domestic animals don't need camouflage. Your wild relatives—"

"I didn't know I had wild relatives!"

"You do, Artie," Merlin said. "You're a pig. You have a scientific name: *Sus scrofa*. There are wild pigs in Europe and Asia that have the same scientific name."

"It's not a very pretty name," grumped Artie. "Can I change it?"

"No, you can't. Besides, it's old and distinguished. It's Latin. *Sus* is the Latin word for pig, and *scrofa* was what the ancient Romans called a mother pig."

Artie was impressed that he now knew some Latin. "So do wild pigs have camouflage?" he asked.

"They do. They're brown or dark

gray or black," said Merlin. "Like me, they're mostly active at night. They can move through the forest or tall grass without being seen. Also, they have sharp tusks, so they can defend themselves."

"Tusks!" exclaimed Artie. "I thought only elephants had tusks. And walruses."

"Members of the pig family have four tusks, two on each side," explained Merlin. "They grow—"

"Pig family!" Artie interrupted. "I didn't know there was a pig family! Who's in my family?" he squealed.

"There are African bush pigs and giant forest hogs and wart hogs and—"

Merlin stopped. He could see that Artie wasn't listening. Artie was trotting around in a circle under Merlin's roost. His tail was as straight as he could make it. It was sticking up like a flag. In fact, it was sticking up like the tail of a wart hog.

"Merlin! Look! Look at me! I'm a wart hog!" he said. "We're in Africa! You be a lion!"

"Okay. What do I have to do?" asked Merlin.

Artie realized that it wouldn't be easy for Merlin to act like a lion. "Well, I guess you can stay up there where you are," said Artie. "Just roar occasionally."

"What will you do?" asked Merlin

"First I'll have a snack," said Artie the wart hog. He carefully bent his front legs so that he was on his knees. He nibbled at the grass.

"What are you eating?" asked Merlin.

"Grass and roots and berries," said Artie, moving forward on his knees.

Suddenly Merlin-the-lion roared. Artie was on his feet instantly. He spun around and backed into a pile of hay.

"Now what's happening?" asked Merlin.

"Now I'm ready to defend myself with my tusks when you attack me," said Artie.

"If I were really a lion and you were really a wart hog and we were really in Africa, would you really hide in a pile of hay?" asked Merlin.

"I'm not hiding! I'm not even *trying* to hide. I'm protecting my flanks. And my rear. Like a good soldier. If I were a real wart hog I'd probably borrow a hole from an aardvark and back into it."

"Artie, it's daytime—" said Merlin.

"Wart hogs are active in daytime," Artie interrupted. "Unlike most wild pigs," he added.

"I know," yawned Merlin. "But lions aren't. And neither are bats. I have to get a good day's sleep so I can hunt tonight."

~ SIX ~

Everyone Is Special

Artie couldn't wait for Merlin to wake up, because he had an important question. As soon as he saw the birds returning to their nests and the sun starting to set, he called out, "Merlin! Merlin! Are there any girl bats?"

"Of course there are," Merlin replied sleepily. "What made you ask that?"

"You're the only bat I know, and you're a boy," Artie replied.

"I had a mother. You had a mother. All mammals have mothers, and all mother mammals are females."

"Oh," said Artie.

"Girls grow up to be women," Merlin continued. "Female piglets grow up to be sows. Young female bats grow up to be—" He stopped, because he didn't know if adult female bats had a special name.

"Grow up to be what?" asked Artie.

"Mothers," said Merlin.

"I remember my mother!" Artie

said. "I remember snuggling close to her and drinking her milk. That was my first food."

"Baby bats nurse, too," said Merlin.

"There were lots of us," Artie said, as more memories flooded back. "I had four brothers and two sisters. We used to push and shove and climb all over each other when we were nursing."

"I didn't have any sisters or brothers," said Merlin. "But I was born in a maternity colony. There were about sixty mothers and sixty babies, all of us hanging from the ceiling of a cave. When our mothers went out to find food for themselves, we would all chirp like birds until they came back to us."

"*Sixty* mothers and *sixty* babies! That's more than a hundred bats all in the same place!" Artie exclaimed. "I can't remember what I was like when I was just born. I know I could wiggle around, but I don't think I could run. Could you fly as soon as you were born, Merlin?"

"No. I had wings, but I didn't know how to use them. I was about a month old before I could fly." Merlin paused and scratched his nose with the little claw on the tip of his wing. "Talking about babies reminds me of something, Artie. Last fall, before I started hibernating, Mrs. P said she'd have some cute babies to show us this spring. I wonder where she is."

Artie thought he heard something rustling the tall grass behind him. He looked over his shoulder, and to his surprise, he saw a familiar face. It was Mrs. P.

"I'm right here," said the opossum. "So are my babies."

Artie couldn't see any baby opossums. "Where are they?" he asked. "Where are your babies? Can you see them, Merlin?"

"Meg. Jo. Beth. Amy. Tom. Huck. Come on out," called Mrs. P. And a minute later, there they were.

"Was that camouflage?" asked Artie, who was still confused.

"No," said Mrs. P. "They were in my pouch. That's where they spend most of their time."

"They're adorable," said Merlin. "They look just like you. How old are they?"

"A little over two months. They're just old enough to start leaving the pouch for a little while every day. Before that, they stayed in my pouch all the time."

"Wasn't that a heavy load of babies to carry around?" asked Merlin.

"They're getting heavy now. But baby opossums are so small when they're born that you could fit twenty of them into a teaspoon."

"Why would anyone want to put baby opossums in a teaspoon?" asked Artie.

"No one would, Artie," said Merlin. "Mrs. P is just trying to give you an idea of how small they were when they were born."

"Oh," said Artie.

"They'll still nurse for another month or two," said Mrs. P. "And then they'll be independent. Come on, kids. Time to go. Do you want to ride on my back or climb back inside?"

"Where are you going?" asked Artie.

"Back to the den. I'll leave the kids there while I go out foraging for food tonight."

After Mrs. P had waddled away, Merlin asked Artie, "Did you notice her tail?"

"It's not very pretty." Artie said. Mrs. P's tail was long, scaly-looking, and hairless. It dragged on the ground behind her.

"You're right. Opossums' tails are not pretty at all. But they are amazingly useful. Mrs. P. can hold onto things with her tail," Merlin told him.

Artie's eyes popped open. "What?" he asked.

"She can wrap it around a branch when she's climbing, and hold on so she doesn't fall," Merlin explained. "A tail like that is called 'prehensile.'"

"Can she pick up her food with it?" asked Artie.

"No. There are some monkeys that can use their tails like hands, but Mrs. P can't do that."

Artie twisted around to try to look at his own tail, but he couldn't even see it. It certainly wasn't useful. "All the mammals we know have something special about them," he sighed. "You can fly. Mrs. P has a pouch and a special tail—and she can play dead. Melissa can stink up the whole world with one squirt from her glands. James has those amazing quills. Folly has the world's best nose, or so she claims. And the longest ears I've ever seen. Is there anything special about me, Merlin?"

"Actually, your snout is special, Artie. No other mammal in the world has a snout like a pig's."

"That's good, I guess, but what is a snout?" Artie asked.

"Your nose. It's round at the end. It's shaped like a disc. No other mammal's nose is like that."

Artie wiggled his nose happily.

"That's not all," Merlin continued. "There's a special bone inside your nose, behind the disc, called a rostral bone. No other mammal has a bone like that. It makes your snout so strong you can dig with it."

"Cool," said Artie. "I'm going to sniff around right now. Maybe I'll smell something I want to dig up."

"And Artie," Merlin added, "When you're rooting around, you can close your nostrils to keep the dirt out."

Merlin looked at Artie, head down and tail up, snorting and snuffling in the dirt. The bat smiled to himself and closed his eyes for his daylong sleep.

~ SEVEN ~

Awake All Night

Artie woke up the next morning with a brilliant idea. He looked up just as Merlin arrived at his day roost in the tree. "I want to stay awake tonight and see your world, Merlin!" he called.

"Okay," replied Merlin. "You'd better nap."

Artie spent a large part of every day napping, but to get ready for his adventure, he snuck in a few extra winks. When dusk came and Merlin woke up, Artie was ready. "Where are we going?" he asked.

"First we'll go to the woods," Merlin said. "There's a nice stream there. We'll both get a drink, and I'll eat a few mosquitoes. I'll fly slowly so you can follow me."

Soon they were in the woods. It was dark, but not too dark, because the moon was almost full. Artie trotted along a path through the trees, following Merlin.

Suddenly Artie saw something white sail over his head. It was about the size and shape of a slice of bread. Then he heard a *whumpf*!

"Merlin!" he shouted. "Do sandwiches fly at night?"

Merlin was so startled he almost crash–landed. "What?" he asked.

"I said, do sandwiches fly at night? I just saw a slice of bread sail past my head. I heard it land, but now I don't see it."

Merlin was shaking his head in puzzlement when a small, shy voice said, "Maybe you saw me."

Artie turned his head toward the voice and saw a tiny gray squirrel on the trunk of a nearby tree. "No, it wasn't you," he said. "What I saw was white. You're gray."

"My belly fur is white," said the squirrel.

"Of course," Merlin laughed. "Artie, this is Becky. She's a flying squirrel. Becky, this is my friend Artie. He's a pig."

"Flying squirrel!" Artie exclaimed. "Merlin, you told me you were the only flying mammal."

"Merlin didn't lie, Artie," Becky said. "I don't fly. I glide."

"What do you mean?" asked Artie.

"I launch myself from a high place

and land in a lower place. Merlin really flies. He can go up and down. I can only go down."

"I'm going to try it!" cried Artie, running to the tree. Artie had wanted to fly since the day he met Merlin. He plopped his front feet on the trunk and gave a few little jumps. But his hooves were slippery. He looked longingly at Becky's tiny claws. She could go up, down, or sideways on the tree trunk. He sighed.

"If you jumped from a high place, Artie, I'm afraid you'd drop like a potato. And land like a mashed potato," Becky said.

"But you don't," said Artie.

"Don't what?" asked Becky.

"Drop like a potato. Is it because you're so small and light?"

"I guess that helps. But it's really because of my gliding membrane. See how loose my skin is?" Becky stretched out her front leg. She looked like she was wearing a very loose, long-sleeved sweater.

Artie couldn't imagine having such loose skin. His skin fitted him exactly. "What does your loose skin do?" he asked.

"When I glide, I stretch all four legs way out," Becky said. She held onto the tree with two legs and stretched out the other two. Artie could see her soft, white belly fur. "My patagium—that's my gliding membrane—spreads out," Becky continued. "I guess I look sort of like a kite."

"Or a piece of bread," murmured Artie.

"The air keeps me up," Becky continued, "and gravity pulls me down. I pick my landing spot, push off, and away I go."

"I wish I could try gliding," Artie said longingly. "But I heard that thump when you landed. That *whumpf*. Does it hurt when you land, Becky?"

"Not really. It's a great way to get

from tree to tree, but I can't pretend I land like a feather," said Becky. "Right before I land I bring all four legs forward, so my patagium forms a little parachute. That slows me down."

"I do more or less the same thing when I land," said Merlin. "I bring my wings forward to slow myself down."

"Becky, are you really a squirrel?" asked Artie.

"I'm a member of the squirrel family," she said. "And I'm a lot like other squirrels. But all of the other squirrels are diurnal."

"Die-what?" asked Artie.

"*Di-ur-nal.* It means active in the daytime. Like you usually are. I'm nocturnal. That means I'm active at night. Like Merlin."

"Speaking of nocturnal," Merlin said, "nocturnal animals eat at night. At least I do. Come on, Artie."

"Okay, I'm coming," Artie said. "Good-bye, Becky." He hated to leave, but Merlin sounded grumpy because he was hungry.

"Stop by on your way home," said Becky. "See that hole up near the top of this tree? It's my nest. It's an empty woodpecker hole. If you don't see me, just holler."

Artie and Merlin set off together toward the stream.

"I just thought of a joke," said Artie. "Knock–knock."

"Who's there?" asked Merlin obligingly.

"Me!" said Artie. "I'm *knock-tur-nal.* Get it?"

Merlin got it.

"You didn't laugh, Merlin," said Artie.

"It's almost impossible to laugh and fly at the same time," said Merlin. "Come on. I'm getting hungrier and hungrier."

~ EIGHT ~

A Deer Friend

Artie was able to follow Merlin through the woods without too much difficulty. Soon they were at the stream. "Oh, good," said Merlin. "My deer friend is here. You can talk to her while I eat a few bites of my dinner."

"I thought *I* was your dear friend," Artie said, but Merlin didn't reply. He had already swung into action. He whizzed back and forth over the water, swooping and twisting and turning. He changed direction without slowing down.

Artie was amazed. He had never seen a bat hunting before. He ran along the bank of the stream looking up at Merlin. The next thing he knew, he was a very wet pig.

To his surprise, Artie found that he could swim. For the first time in his life, he felt light instead of heavy. "This must be what flying feels like," he thought, paddling in circles.

When Artie waded out of the water, he found himself nose-to-nose with a tall animal with beautiful big brown eyes.

"I'm Merlin's friend," the animal said. "My name is Diana. I'm a white-tailed deer."

"I'm Artie," Artie said. He shook the water out of his ears. "I'm a pig. That was my first swim. I loved it. I felt so light!"

"I'm sure you did," said Diana

sternly. "But you muddied the water for everyone who's here to drink."

"Oh, I'm sorry," Artie said. "I really am. I fell in by accident while I was watching Merlin. I never saw him flying that way before."

"He always flies like that when he's hunting," Diana replied. "When he zeroes in on a bug, that bug is history."

Diana was a lot taller than Artie. His neck was getting stiff from looking up at her. He wiggled his neck in a circle to loosen it, and suddenly he saw Diana's feet. "You have hooves!" he said. "Can you climb trees?"

"With hooves?" Diana laughed. "I

doubt it. You and I are artiodactyls, Artie. But I can't stay here and talk. I have to go back to my fawns." She turned to go.

"Wait!" called Artie. "Diana, you said you're a white-tailed deer. Your tail isn't white!"

Diana smiled and flicked her tail up. The underside was white. Then with one bound, she disappeared silently into the trees.

Artie charged into the underbrush after her—and crashed into Diana, who had stopped next to a tree. "*Oompf!*" she gasped.

Merlin flew up and roosted in the tree over Diana's head. "Artie," he scolded, "you're noisier than a bear."

"I just wanted to see the fawns," said Artie.

"It's lucky you didn't step on them!" said Diana. Then she added more gently, "All right. Follow me. But tiptoe."

There they were, two tiny deer curled up like two little spotted balls in a nest of leaves and grass.

"Oh," breathed Artie. "Oh."

"They're twins," Diana whispered.

"They're beautiful," Artie whispered back. "Will they wake up soon?"

Two little heads came up. Four bright eyes looked at Artie. Then the fawns stretched and stood up. They were taller than Artie, even though they were only a month old. They immediately started to nurse.

"I nurse them three or four times a day," said Diana. "They're just beginning to eat grass."

"They're big!" said Artie.

"They already weigh three times as much as they did when they were born," said Diana proudly.

"Follow me back to the stream, Artie," said Merlin. "You can talk to Diana again later."

"Okay," whispered Artie. "Bye, Diana. Bye, babies."

As Artie trotted along, he thought about what Diana had said. "Merlin," he called, "Diana said I'm an Artie–something, and she is, too. But her name isn't Artie. What did she say?"

"She said that you're both *artie-oh-dack-tills*. It means you both have hooves and an even number of toes. If you could see the bones inside your leg, Artie, you'd see that you actually have four toes. You walk on two of them. Cows and goats and antelopes and giraffes are artiodactyls, too."

Artie was amazed. "How about the horse?" he asked. "She has hooves."

"You're right. She does. But her hoof isn't divided. She actually walks on one toe." Merlin paused. "Did you know a hoof is just an overgrown toenail?" he asked.

Artie scratched his nose with one of his overgrown toenails. "Good grief," he sighed. "Merlin, does that mean your claws are toenails, too?"

"Well, yes," the bat answered.

"If my hooves were shaped

differently, we could hang around together!" Artie exclaimed.

As they made their way back to the stream, Artie thought of another question. "When you're flying around in the dark trying to catch beetles and mosquitoes to eat, how can you see them?" he asked Merlin.

"Remember Little Red Riding Hood?" asked Merlin.

"Yes...?" replied Artie.

"Remember what Little Red Riding Hood said to the wolf? She said, 'What big ears you have, Grandmother.' Say it to me."

"What big ears you have, Grandmother Merlin," giggled Artie.

"The better to hear *myself* with," Merlin said. "I don't have to see my prey. I use echolocation."

"What you use is lots of big words," said Artie.

"Echolocation? That's not so big. You know what an echo is, don't you?" asked Merlin.

"I guess I do. Yes, I do."

"And you know what location means, too. It's a place where something is. When I'm hunting, I make very high-pitched sounds. The sound waves hit the insect I'm hunting and bounce back to me. Even if the insect is flying through the bushes, I know exactly where it is. That's echolocation. It's like radar."

"You're amazing, Merlin," Artie sighed.

Merlin smiled. "All bats are, I think. Follow me, Artie."

NINE

The Mole National Anthem

When they got back to the stream, Artie waded in for a drink. To the pig's surprise, Merlin drank without landing. He just swooped low enough to dip his chin into the water. Diana came back and she drank, too. The stream was a popular place, day and night. It was quiet and peaceful.

But wait—did Artie hear someone singing?

"Twinkle, twinkle, little mole,
Time to dig another hole."

Artie cocked his head and listened. He heard it again. And again. He looked at Diana.

"It's the mole," she said. "I call him Twinkle, because he sings that song all the time. Over and over. I think it's the Mole National Anthem."

Artie walked closer to the sound. The small black animal lifted his head.

Artie gasped in surprise. "Excuse

me," he said. "I think you have something stuck on your nose."

"That *is* my nose," said the mole huffily. He turned around and shuffled slowly toward a hole in the bank of the stream.

"Twinkle, I'm sorry!" said Artie. "I didn't know."

The mole turned around. "You can call me Twinkle," he said. "Diana does. But I prefer Chris."

"If Chris is your name, I'll call you Chris," said Artie.

"It's part of my name," replied Chris. "Part of my *scientific* name," he added proudly. "I might have a funny face, but I have a beautiful scientific name."

"What is it?" asked Artie.

"*Condylura cristata*," the mole said. "*Con-dee-lure-ah chris-ta-ta*," he repeated.

Artie was jealous. He didn't much

like his own scientific name, *Sus scrofa*, but Merlin had told him he couldn't change it.

"Does it mean something?" asked Artie.

"It means somebody made a mistake, a big mistake," said Chris. "But I don't mind, since I love the name."

Merlin flew over to listen.

"Look at my tail." Chris turned slowly around so that Artie, Merlin, and Diana could see it. His tail was long, straight, and scaly. It was thinly covered with black hairs. There didn't seem to be anything special about it.

"*Condylura* comes from two Greek words that mean 'knobby tail,'" the mole explained. "Some early explorer in North America sent a drawing of a star-nosed mole—that's what I am—to scientists in Europe. They had never seen a star-nosed mole. There aren't any in Europe."

Artie's eyes got wide. "But your tail isn't bumpy!" he exclaimed.

"I know," Chris replied. "That's the strange part. For some reason, the drawing showed a lumpy, bumpy tail. It looked like a string of beads. It was so unusual, scientists made 'knobby-tail' part of my name."

"How about the *cristata* part?" asked Merlin.

"That's for my nose," replied Chris.

"Your nose doesn't look like a star," commented Artie. "It looks like—I don't know what it looks like."

"It *is* unusual," said Diana.

"I know," said Chris proudly, wiggling his twenty-two pink nasal rays. "No other mammal has anything like it. *Cristata* means 'tufted' or 'crested.'"

"Crested knobby-tail," said Diana. "That's better than my scientific name, Chris. Mine's *Odocoileus virginianus*. It means 'hollow tooth from Virginia.'"

"Better than mine, too. Mine's

Eptesicus fuscus. 'Dusky house flyer.'" muttered Merlin. "Can you imagine?"

"I can't imagine," said Artie. "I wish we could find out why you and Diana have such strange scientific names. Can we ask those scientists?"

"No, they lived a really long time ago," Diana said. She lowered her head to look at Chris. "Why do you sing about digging all the time?" she asked.

"Because that's what I do for a living," Chris explained.

Artie looked from Diana's long legs to his own short ones, and then at the mole's. "You don't seem to have much in the way of legs," he commented. "How do you dig?"

Chris waggled a front paw. "My front feet make perfect shovels."

Artie and Diana leaned down to look. The mole's front feet were as wide as they were long, and his claws were huge. Chris's feet were remarkably different from the two artiodactyls' hooves. They were even more different from Merlin's wing, with its one tiny claw.

"How amazing that we're all mammals!" Artie thought.

~ TEN ~

A Predator

Suddenly, silently, an owl swooped down.

Artie shuddered and closed his eyes. When he opened them, the mole was gone.

"Oh, poor Chris," wailed Artie. "Where is he? Did the owl catch him?"

"No," Diana reassured Artie. "Chris

went underwater. I'm sure he'll be back in a minute or two. The owl will have to eat something else for dinner tonight."

"I hate predators," Artie murmured.

"I'm a predator," said Merlin softly.

Artie stared at Merlin. "What do you mean?" he asked.

"I prey on bugs," Merlin explained.

"Oh, that's not really being a predator," Artie said.

"The bugs think it is," Merlin told him.

Just then the mole surfaced. "We were lucky that time, Merlin," he said.

"Why was Merlin lucky?" asked Artie. "He just said he was a predator."

"I'm both," said Merlin. "I'm both predator and prey. I prey on insects, but some bigger predators prey on bats. Owls do. There is even a kind of bat that eats other bats, but it doesn't live around here."

Artie shuddered. He decided it was time to change the subject. "I'm a good swimmer," he said. "I do the piggy-paddle. But I never swam underwater. What's it like down there, Chris?"

"Wet," said Chris. "And dark."

"Is it scary?" asked Artie.

"Not for me," replied Chris. "I spend lots of time underwater. One of my tunnels opens underwater. But basically, I'm fossorial."

"You're what?" asked Artie.

"A digger. Adapted for digging. For living underground. 'Fossorial' comes from the same word as 'fossil.'"

"There's another predator," said Merlin, looking across the stream. It was the raccoon.

"Oh, noooo...," exclaimed Artie.

Diana smiled. "Don't worry, Artie. You and I are much too big to have to worry about owls or raccoons. And Merlin's safe. Raccoons can't fly."

"Raccoons can't fly, but they do prey on bats from time to time," said Merlin. "Artie, we have more exploring to do tonight. Ready to go?"

"Sure," Artie said happily. "I'm ready. Where are we going next, Merlin?"

~ ELEVEN ~

Busy Beavers

Where *would* they go? Merlin thought about all the things he wanted to show Artie. He turned to the pig and asked, "Do you think you're a good enough swimmer to swim upstream a ways and meet the beaver family?"

"I'll try," said Artie. "If I get tired, can I climb out on the bank and rest?"

"Sure," Merlin replied. The bat let

go of the branch he was hanging from, dropped a few inches to gain air speed, and flew slowly above the stream. Artie was able to follow him easily.

Artie trotted along where the water was shallow and swam through a few deep places. It was a warm night. The cool water felt wonderful on his skin.

"Climb out here, Artie," called Merlin. "We're almost at the beavers' dam."

Artie scrambled onto the bank of the stream. Just as he did, there was a tremendous crash. A tree fell only about three pig-lengths in front of him.

"Rats!" shouted Merlin angrily. "That was one of my favorite trees!"

"Rats?" asked Artie.

"That was just an expression," said Merlin. "Actually it was the beavers."

"I don't understand," said Artie.

"They cut that tree down. They gnawed right through the trunk with their big front teeth," Merlin explained.

"But why?" Artie asked.

"To build their dam," Merlin replied.

"You said a bad word, Merlin," said Artie. "That's the second time you said it."

"I did not say a bad word," Merlin replied. "Look right in front of you. See all those sticks in the water? See how they are keeping the water from flowing? That's a dam. That's the kind of dam I was talking about."

Artie stared. On the far side of the dam, the stream had become a pond. The moon shone on the water. It was beautiful. The longer Artie looked, the more he could see. He saw a round, dark head swimming toward the dam. Near it, a leafy branch moved slowly through the water.

Artie walked closer to the edge of the pond, slipped on the mud—and slid into the pond with a splash. Just before

his head went under, he heard a very
loud sound. Was it thunder?

Artie bobbed right up to the
surface, shook his head to clear his
eyes and ears, and waddled out onto
the bank. "Merlin!" he
gasped. "What was that
noise?"

"It was a danger
signal—" Merlin
replied.

Artie dove headfirst under a bush. All Merlin could see was a curly pink tail.

"What danger?" Artie squealed from his hiding place.

"You. You startled the beavers when you fell in. The father beaver slapped his tail on the water to warn his family."

"He must have quite a tail," said Artie. As he wiggled backwards out of his hiding place, he wondered if he could run backwards. He had never tried. "Merlin," he asked, "can you fly backwards?"

"Only frontwards," said Merlin. "Look, Artie, the beavers are coming over. I told them you weren't dangerous. You can apologize for scaring them."

Artie saw five heads moving smoothly through the water toward him. One by one, five furry animals climbed out of the water. They waddled up the bank and shook themselves, showering water droplets all around.

"We're the beaver family," said one of the large beavers. "I'm Mother Beaver."

"I'm Artie," said Artie. "I'm sorry I startled you."

"No problem," said the other large beaver. "It's easy enough for us to dive under. In fact, it's good practice for the kits. When I slap my tail, they're supposed to dive immediately."

"We did!" The three little beavers were so excited about escaping from danger that they tried to jump up and down, but beavers can't jump.

"They did," said Merlin. "I was watching them." He looked around. "This is good hunting territory," he said. "I'll be back in a little while." Merlin flew over the pond, darting and twisting as he snatched insects from the air.

Artie and the beavers watched Merlin hunting for a minute or two. Then another dome-shaped pile of sticks caught Artie's eye. "Why did you build

another dam in the middle of the pond?"
he asked.

"We didn't," said Father Beaver.
"That's our lodge. That's where we live."

"Is the door on the other side?"
asked Artie.

"No, it's underwater," Mother
Beaver explained.

"You spend a lot of time
underwater," Artie commented.

"We can stay underwater for five
minutes at a time!" one of the little
beavers told Artie.

"We'll swim under the ice this winter," his sister added.

Their brother said, "Today we're helping Mom and Dad take sticks to the lodge."

Suddenly Artie had an idea. "I can swim, too," he said. "But not underwater. Let's race."

"Okay," said Father Beaver. "You and the kits. Over to the lodge and back."

"This will be fun," Mother Beaver said. "Ready, Artie? Ready, kits? GO!"

In the blink of an eye, Artie and Mother and Father Beaver were alone together. Artie was up to his knees in the water, and the big beavers were watching from the shore. The three kits were almost at the lodge.

"How did they do that?" asked Artie.

"They were born to swim," said Mother Beaver. "Beavers have webbed hind feet." She showed Artie her hind foot. "You're much faster on land, though."

The little beavers swam back looking pleased with themselves, and Merlin flew back looking full and contented.

"We should get back to work," said Mother Beaver. "You know what they say—busy as a beaver!" The beaver family said good-bye and swam off toward their lodge.

"Did you know that I can run faster than a beaver?" Artie asked as he followed Merlin back downstream.

"I sort of thought you could," replied Merlin. He led the way back to Artie's yard and his day roost. They were both tired—happy but tired.

"I had no idea there was so much happening in the woods at night," Artie sighed as they both settled down to sleep.

~ TWELVE ~

Merlin's Dream

Soon Artie was snoring gently, dreaming about the fawns and beaver kits and that funny little mole. His nose twitched.

Artie dreamed on. He dreamed that he and Merlin were in Africa, where there are elephants, and in Australia, where there are kangaroos and wombats. He and Merlin always had fun together. Merlin liked answering his questions and explaining things. What would their next adventure be?

Merlin folded his wings and soon he, too, was asleep. Strangely enough, he was smiling in his sleep. Could it be that he was dreaming, too? Yes, he was!

Merlin was dreaming that Artie had grown huge wings. Not wings with feathers, like a bird's. Not bat wings. Artie had *pig* wings! He and Artie were flying together in the moonlight! It was a wonderful dream. Merlin loved exploring with Artie, because Artie was curious and eager to learn. He loved to see new places and make new friends. Where would they go next?

THE END

Fact or Fiction?

Fact underlies the fiction in *Artie and Merlin*, except for this: as far as we know, humans are the only mammals that talk to each other, tell jokes, and can imagine situations they have never experienced.

Mammals send and receive messages in many ways. They may squeak, purr, chatter, hiss, snarl, or whine. They may stamp their feet and wag or slap their tails. Most mammals use their noses to identify friends and avoid strangers. They send signals with their bodies, too, sometimes by rearing up and making their hair stand on end to look large and fierce, and sometimes by crouching down or rolling over to apologize or say they do not want to fight. A skunk's black and white coat, the very opposite of camouflage, is a kind of signal. It warns other mammals to keep their distance. This works for adult animals, if not for young ones, who have to learn from experience. Some skunks even do handstands to say, "Keep away or I'll spray!"

Meet the Mammals

Merlin is a big brown bat. "Big" is a relative term: the largest big brown bats weigh less than an ounce (about 23 g). In flight, their wingspan is about a foot, so they are about the size of small birds. They often make their homes near people, on farms, in towns, and even in cities. They roost in hollow trees, buildings, or caves. Big brown bats live in every US state except Alaska and Hawaii. Their range extends well into

Canada and south through Mexico and beyond.

Like other insect-eating bats, big brown bats leave the roost around sunset. They may fly a mile or more, at speeds up to 20 miles (33 km) an hour, to forage for food. They especially like flying beetles. A female bat that is nursing her young may eat her own weight in insects every night. In eastern North America, big brown bats usually have twins; in the West, they usually have just one baby. Big brown bats are born in maternity colonies. Their mothers hang the babies close together, and they keep each other warm. Bats live much longer than other small mammals:

big brown bats can live to be 19 years old in the wild.

Merlin's tail is almost completely inside his tail membrane. Some species of bats have long tails that stick out beyond the membrane. Some have tails that poke out the top. A few species have no tail at all. Bats' wings are made of two thin layers of skin stretched over their arm and hand bones.

Artie is a young pig, curious and eager to learn. Like all pigs, he spends much of each day sleeping or dozing. Sometimes he is in a state called REM (rapid eye movement) sleep. When we humans are in REM sleep, we dream. Pigs probably dream, too. However, Artie almost certainly cannot dream about or imagine something he has never experienced, like being a wart hog.

Pigs are intelligent. Scientists tested how well different domestic animals did in finding their way through mazes. Dogs did well. Chickens and horses worked their way slowly through the maze. Sheep got confused. They milled around and never finished. Cats refused to participate. Pigs were the best problem solvers of all the animals tested.

Artie and Diana are both artiodactyls, hoofed mammals with an even number of toes. So are camels, sheep, goats, antelopes, giraffes and hippos. Horses, rhinos and tapirs are

perissodactyls (per-iss-oh-dack-tills),
hoofed mammals with an odd number of
toes.

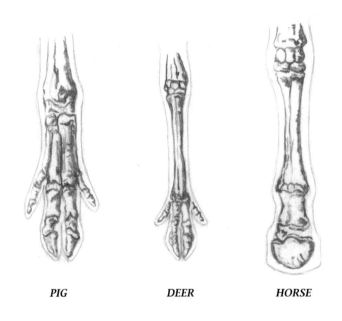

PIG   DEER   HORSE

Folly was Sue Ruff's beloved pet
bloodhound. She lived with Sue and her
family in Washington, D.C. She really

did find an opossum in the yard, carry it around in her mouth, and put it down without hurting it. She really was sprayed by a skunk when she was a puppy. She also met a porcupine in the woods and had to have its quills pulled out of her nose.

If...

If you and a bat were almost the same size, and you could see x-rays of your bones and the bat's bones, you would be amazed.

Your upper arm and a bat's are very

similar, and they attach to your shoulder very similarly. Your forearms, from the elbow to the wrist, and a bat's, are also very much alike. You and the bat both have four fingers and a thumb.

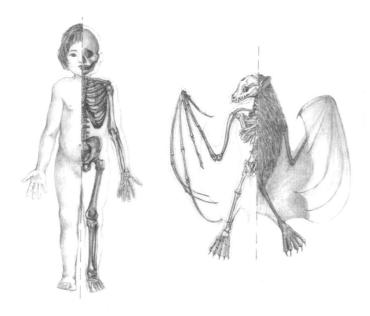

Here's where things get interesting. A bat's fingers are much longer than its forearm, because they support its wing membrane. When the bat folds its wings, they fold back. You cannot bend your wrist the way a bat does when it folds its wings.

You and the bat both have short thumbs, but a bat's thumbs are much shorter than yours. On page 5, you can see Merlin's thumb sticking out on the tip of his wing when he is flying. Merlin only has one "fingernail," a short claw on his thumb.

Look at Merlin roosting on page 43. His tummy is against the trunk. His knees bend away from the trunk. Bend your knees: Merlin's bend the other way!

Also, he can bend his neck so far back that he can see behind himself.

When a bat roosts, it does not have to think about holding on with its back claws. It holds on automatically. It has to decide to let go.

Explore More

Merlin, Mrs. P, Melissa, James, Becky, Diana, Twinkle (Chris), and the beavers are all North American mammals. So are foxes and raccoons. You can find photographs, drawings, and maps showing where they live, and you can hear what some of these mammals sound like, on a free Smithsonian website, www.mnh.si.edu/mna.

Artie and Folly are not on the North American Mammals website because they are domestic mammals.

There are more than 1,000 species of bats worldwide. The Bat Conservation International website, www.batcon. org, has wonderful pictures and great information about these amazing mammals.

The website www.ultimateungulate. com offers information about all the hoofed mammals of the world.

Many zoos have excellent websites,

and there are hundreds of good books about mammals.

Animals that are very different from each other can be friends. Read about the friendship between a young hippopotamus, Owen, and a 130-year-old tortoise, Mzee, in two books by Isabella Hatkoff, *Owen & Mzee: The True Story of a Remarkable Friendship* (2006) and *Owen & Mzee: The Language of Friendship* (2007).

Sue Ruff, a Washington, D.C., writer and editor, has volunteered for many years at the Smithsonian's National Zoo. With Don E. Wilson, she co-edited The Smithsonian Book of North American Mammals.

Don E. Wilson is a Senior Scientist, Curator of Mammals, and Chairman of the Department of Vertebrate Zoology at the Smithsonian's National Museum of Natural History. His 37 years there have been spent studying mammals all around the world.

Lolette Guthrie is an artist living and working in Chapel Hill, North Carolina. Always a painter, Lolette has also been an elementary school teacher, an art teacher, and an environmental educator.

Don and Sue are long-time collaborators on books about mammals for both children and adults. Sue and Lolette have been friends since their student days at Swarthmore College. All three love animals, children's books, and reading with their grandchildren.